The Christmas Car-Sled Race

Adapted by **Annie Auerbach**

Based on the episode by **Krystal Banzon**

Illustrated by **Character Building Studio**

DISNEP PRESS

Los Angeles • New York

SUSTAINABLE FORESTRY INITIATIVE

Certified Sourcing

www.sfiprogram.org

SFI-01415

The SFI label applies to the text stock

With Christmas only a few days away, Bo still doesn't know what to get his father, Chief Bayani, for the holiday. "I can't give him socks again," Bo complains to Flash.

But Flash isn't listening. He is too busy looking at the **_Frostbite 5000_** in the store window. It is a top-of-the-line car sled.

Just then, Mayor Geno and Chief Bayani walk up. The mayor asks Bo if he is going to enter this year's *Christmas car-sled race*.

"We would if we had a car sled," says Bo.

"If we had that car sled," Flash adds, pointing to the awesome Frostbite 5000.

"You don't need a fancy car sled to race," says Chief Bayani. "You could use my old Snow Rocket sled."

"Perfect," says the mayor. "Because the prize this year is a *parol*. It's a beautiful Filipino star lantern. This one is special. It is made with capiz shells."

Chief Bayani gasps. "I've always wanted one of those."

Bo whispers to Flash. "I know the **perfect gift** for my dad: the *parol!* We're going to win that race to get it!"

It's race day! Bo and his dad have fixed up the Snow Rocket. Flash drives onto the sled, and the bindings click into place.

As they head toward the starting line, they spot the other Firebuds. Jayden has designed a slick, high-tech car sled for him and Piston to use. Violet and Axl have a colorful snowboard as their car sled.

Then Bo sees Iggy and Rod . . . and they have the Frostbite 5000.
"What's up, Firebuds?" says Iggy.
Piston is worried that the horn on the Frostbite 5000 is too loud.
"It could set off an *avalanche*," he says.

"An avalanche is when a ton of snow rushes down the mountain and covers everything in its path," Piston explains.

Iggy shakes his head. "Maybe the snow would catch you. But not us. We're too fast."

Nearby, June and Vance, her camera-van *vroom*-mate, begin filming the big race.

"Hola, JuneTube viewers," she says.

They drive up a snowy hill to get a better view of the starting line.

Mayor Geno stands in front of a microphone. "Welcome, everyone, to Gearbox Grove's world-famous **Christmas Car-Sled Race**! On your marks, get set, **SLED**!"

The competitors race downhill, with Bo and Flash quickly taking the lead. But Iggy and Rod speed toward a snowdrift, leap off it, and fly right over Bo and Flash.

Now Iggy and Rod are in the lead! They **blast** their horn in victory.

HONK!

Rumble, *rumble!* AVALANCHE!
Just as Piston predicted, the loud horn causes a wall
of snow to rush down the mountain!

Luckily, the Firebuds, Iggy, and Rod are all okay.

But June and Vance are trapped in the snow.
"Help!" calls Vance.

Bo springs into action. "We need a **rescue plan**!"

"But you need to finish the race so you can win the *parol* for your dad," Flash reminds him.

"Don't worry," Piston tells Bo. "We'll rescue June and Vance. Go back to the race."

"Okay . . . thanks, Firebuds," says Bo.

Bo sees Iggy and Rod already back in the race, then he looks toward June and Vance. He really wants to win the race, but he can't leave without helping first.

   "Huddle up, Firebuds!" Bo says.

Working together, the Firebuds rescue June and Vance. "You **saved** us!" says June. "Thanks, Firebuds!"

"What a rescue!" Chief Bayani says proudly. Bo smiles, but then he hears cheers from the crowd. Iggy and Rod have won the race.

"I, uh, have to go do some last-minute Christmas shopping," Bo says to his dad. "See you at home."

"What's up with Bo?" Chief Bayani asks the others after Bo leaves.

"He's disappointed he lost the race," explains Violet. "He wanted to win that *parol* so he could give it to you for Christmas."

"Oh . . ." said Chief Bayani. He is touched that his son hoped to win the prize for him.

On Christmas Eve, everyone gathers around the Christmas tree. Bo hands his dad a gift. It's a pair of socks—with *parols* on them! The chief smiles. He **_loves_** Bo's gift.

"I wanted to give you something else," says Bo, "but I couldn't get it."
"The present I want isn't fancy or fine," his dad tells him.
"Spending time with you is the *perfect gift*."

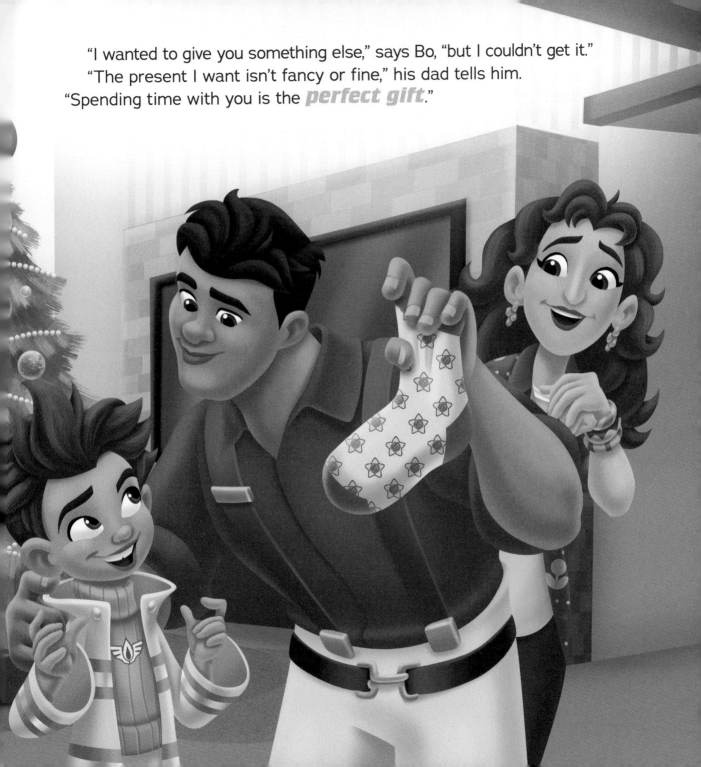

Chief Bayani leads Bo into the workshop and pulls out bamboo and colored paper. Then he shows Bo how to make their very own *parols*—together. It truly is a **merry Christmas**.

Happy holidays from all the Firebuds!